HOW TO LIVE TWICE

Ricardo Camino

HOW TO LIVE TWICE

ISBN Softcover 978-1-991299-07-9
ISBN ePub 978-1-991299-15-4

Typeset in Garamond.

Cataloguing in Publishing Data
Title: How To Live Twice
Author: Ricardo Camino
Subjects: Christian Living; Christian Fiction; Short Stories; Faith and Spirituality

A copy of this title is held at the National Library of New Zealand.

To R. P. W.

My star.

CONTENTS

CHAPTER ONE

"Up your flaming jumper, Adams! I'm fed up to the back teeth with your unending criticism of my work," the painter shouted as he hurled his paint brush onto the ground at Gunther Adam's feet.

Gunther stepped back quickly and checked his boots for paint splatters.

"Find yourself another painter who will tolerate your constant microscopic judgmentalism—if that's possible! I'm leaving. I hope to high heaven that I'll never see your face again!" Chris yelled as he turned away and stomped off.

Half an hour later, Tom Price tapped Gunther on the shoulder.

"What?"

"The boss wants to see you. Now! He's thoroughly ticked off about something. If I were you, I wouldn't keep him waiting."

Gunther put his tools into his carpenter's carry box and, leaving it on a corner of the deck he was building, set off towards the boss's shed, massaging a dab of lanolin skin crème into his work-hardened palms as he went.

"You want to see me, Jim?"

"Yes, Gunther. Please sit down."

James Grant, Gunther's boss, spoke first. "Gunther, I value you as an employee for I never have to check the quality of your work. You are a perfectionist. However, Gunther, your perfectionism has made you intolerant of other workers on site, be they carpenters, plasterers, floor-sanders, or painters. I had a good painter leave today, vowing he'll never return as long as you are on the team here. When I asked him, 'Why?' Chris said he's sick and tired of your continual grizzling about a couple of small paint spots here, or an almost invisible unpainted streak there. He told me that you said to him, 'Doctors can bury their mistakes, chum, but you can't. So, *don't* make any!'

"What am I to do Gunther? I'm tearing my hair out. I don't want to lose you, mate, for you are an excellent tradesman. It's just that you rile your workmates with your unrelenting and meddling fastidiousness. I've spoken to you about this more than once. It seems to me, however, that you value your own opinions more than you value your relationship with me and the other workers.

"After doing a SWOT analysis of this on-going problem, I've come to a conclusion: You have a month's paid holiday leave due, which I'll extend to six weeks if you will spend two of those weeks with this professional counsellor," Jim said, handing Gunther the counsellor's card.

"What for?"

"He's a life coach who will help you become a more tolerant and considerate person; not so insufferably picky. If you become a kinder, more forbearing person, Gunther, one day you'll make a great overseer. But that won't happen until there's a considerable improvement in the way you treat your fellow workers."

"Who will pay the counsellor's fees?"

"If you give me your word that you will do this course, the company will. Once you've finished the porch railings, take the rest of the day off, and let me know your decision first thing tomorrow morning."

Gunther, a controlling choleric with no close friends, tossed and turned on his bed most of the night, sleeping very little. The next morning, realising he had no other acceptable option, he told his boss that he would be willing to meet with the life coach for as long as was necessary.

***

Peter Gordon, a retired clergyman from New Zealand who lived in one of Brisbane's leafy suburbs, was expecting Gunther, having been told about the problem by James Grant.

Peter shook hands with Gunther and invited him into his study.

"Tell me," Peter asked, "Are you a Christian?"

"Sort of," Gunther replied with a shrug.

"What do you mean by 'sort of'?"

"While still living at home, my father would ask us to bow our heads before eating breakfast and dinner, and he'd pray, 'For what we are about to receive, Lord make us truly thankful. Amen.'"

"Did you go to church?"

"Our church was a mausoleum."

"A mausoleum?"

"Yes. It was full of mostly spiritually dead people, put to sleep by ritualistic and boring services."

"What do you mean by *mostly* spiritually dead people?"

"There were some genuine Christians there, hanging on by their fingernails. Our denomination's mission was to get outsiders to join us and become just like we were. I didn't see any future in that."

"Were there many young people in your church?"

"I was the last, and I also left."

"Not good," responded the counsellor. Then he continued. "Gunther, there is another man, Trevor, about your age, who also grew up in a family that had just a modicum of Christianity. He too has relationship issues that need to be addressed and will be coming to see me for counselling every Monday to Thursday evening between seven and eight. Would that schedule suit you?"

"You run *night* classes?"

"Yes. I do so for clients who cannot come during the day."

Gunther smiled. Perhaps if his counselling sessions were at that hour he might be allowed to continue working during the day.

***

The next morning Gunther asked his boss for permission to continue working during the day, while attending night evening classes with the counsellor.

Jim stood there with his arms folded and a dubious smile on his face as Gunther presented this option.

"I'll tell you what I'll do," Jim offered after considering Gunther's suggestion. "You may continue working here while you attend your evening counselling sessions with Peter Gordon. But just one genuine complaint from another worker about your interference, and you'll be given the boot. Do you hear me?"

"Yes Boss. Thank you, Jim. Thank you," Gunther said as he turned to leave.

"Gunther!" called Jim. "If you have a problem with someone else's work, just zip your lips and tell me. I'm the boss here. Not you. By the way, Gunther, Winston Churchill said something that you, especially, should heed."

"What was that?"

"Churchill said, 'Life is fraught with opportunities to keep your mouth shut.'"

CHAPTER TWO

In the hot evening air, Gunther and Trevor introduced themselves to each other at Peter Gordon's front gate. Both young men, a little apprehensive, went up the path to the house for their first session, serenaded by a pair of barking owls in a silky oak just inside the hedge on the eastern boundary of Peter's front yard.

Trevor knocked on the door and stepped back.

The door opened. "Come in, come in," welcomed Peter with a disarming smile. He ushered them to two chairs in his well-lit office.

Peter sat opposite them at a plain wooden table.

On the table, in front of Peter and each of the two men, was a dark blue glossy paperback *Contemporary English New Testament*, also known as the *Bible for Today's Family*, together with a writing pad and a ballpoint pen.

"Firstly," said Peter, "I'd like you to tell me your full names and something about yourselves, perhaps your achievements and hobbies?

When he looked expectantly at Trevor, Trev began. "I am Trevor Hudson Davis, and I have a Bachelor of Science degree, sir. I'm currently working in Research and Development in the lab at Westcott's paint factory. And my hobby is bird watching."

"A twitcher?"

"Yes."

"Your favourite bird?"

"That would have to be the lyrebird."

"The great imitator. How passionate are you about searching for birds that are new to you?"

"I recently purchased a pair of Audubon binoculars that enable me to identify the different coloured leg bands on birds at a distance," Trevor replied.

"Wonderful. You, Gunther?"

"I am Gunther Arthur Adams, and I am an indentured carpenter, sir, employed by the Cornerstone Construction Company. My foreman is James Grant. And my hobby is making wooden toys, and stuff like that."

"What kind of toys?"

"Rocking horses mainly. My best-selling model has a realistic head with glass eyes, a mane, and a tail. It also has a leather saddle with stirrups. It's not cheap, but I have enough orders to keep me busy for some time."

"Impressive. Thank you. Now let's tackle the reason why you're both here. I understand that you've come to see me today because you are handicapped by bad habits that you wish to overcome. Is that correct?"

Gunther and Trevor nodded.

Once I've assessed the underlying cause for your bad habits I'll know what should be done to help you eliminate them."

"Here is a questionnaire," Peter said, "with a list of questions for you to mark with a tick or cross. They are very basic and will only take a short time to fill in."

***

After checking their answers Peter, said, "Okay. It is my assessment that while you both have high self-esteem, you also have very low self-worth."

"What's the difference, sir?"

"The leader of a motorcycle gang has high self-esteem because he's the boss," replied Peter. "But he has low self-worth because of the bad things he does."

"So, it's not wrong to have high self-esteem?" asked Trevor.

"Definitely not! But self-worth is much better. And you both are lacking in self-worth."

"Okay," said Trevor. "What do we need to do to improve our self-worth?"

"You need to understand the value that God puts on you."

"So, what are we worth in God's eyes?"

"You are each like a small velvet covered box that a young man passes to his beloved when he proposes to her. With great joy and expectation, she opens it, only to discover that it's empty. You, too, are like that empty box."

"Empty of what?"

"The Spirit of Jesus," said Peter. "Without the Spirit of Jesus in you, you are just empty vessels."

"As you well know, sir, most people don't believe in Jesus," said Trevor. "In fact, I'm not sure about him either. Is there any proof that he actually existed?"

"Trevor, in that blue paperback New Testament in front of you is more than enough evidence to convince an intelligent individual like you that Jesus is a real person who lived in Israel a bit over 2000 years ago. In that small volume are records of his life and teachings by his disciples: Matthew, Mark, and John.

"Luke, a physician from Antioch in Syria, after interviewing people who had heard Jesus speak and had seen what he did, wrote the fourth Gospel about a decade after Matthew, Mark, and John. Luke's Gospel also has some of Jesus' teachings that Matthew, Mark, and John don't have in their Gospels.

"Additionally, your New Testament also contains several books by a former rabid anti-Christian, Saul of Tarsus, who later adopted the Roman name of Paul. Saul had a face-to-face life-changing encounter with the resurrected Jesus. After that encounter, he wrote most of the books in the New Testament.

"That's five good witnesses."

"Sir," interrupted Gunther. "How do you know these writers didn't collaborate in a joint effort to make up this story about a Jesus?"

"That didn't happen because, while their records of Jesus' life and teachings contain much that is the same, each of these Gospel writers also provides information about Jesus that is not found in the other Gospels. Finally, the evidence that best undergirds the truth about Jesus is his resurrection from the dead."

"Someone rising from the dead stretches belief to the breaking point, sir. What evidence is there that Jesus actually rose from the dead?"

"Well, when Jesus was crucified, several people, identified in Mark 15:40-41, stood at his cross and waited there until he died. Furthermore, the Roman senator and historian, Tacitus, also affirmed that Christos (the Roman word for Christ or Messiah) suffered the extreme penalty under Pontius Pilate. Then, after Jesus died on the cross, his body was taken down by two sympathetic members of the Sanhedrin— Joseph of Arimathea and Nicodemus—and placed in a tomb belonging to Joseph. So, the proof for Jesus' death, is, therefore, very substantial.

"Now, about his resurrection: After the Jewish leaders had Jesus crucified, his twelve disciples, fearing they'd be the next on their list to be executed, hid themselves behind locked doors in a second storey room (John 20:19). A few days later, Jesus, who had risen from the dead, came to them. Thinking they were seeing an apparition of Jesus, they were scared out of their wits. Having a dead person turn up in your house would be chilling, to say the least.

"So, to prove that he was a real person, Jesus said, 'A spirit doesn't have a physical body as I have.' Holding out his hands he said, 'Check for yourselves. 'Here, touch the nail marks in my wrists and feel this scar in my side.' When they shrunk back, Jesus asked them for a piece of cooked fish, which he ate in their presence, finally convincing them that he was a real person and had truly risen from the dead. (Luke 24:36-43).

"After this astounding face-to-face encounter with their resurrected Lord, the disciples rose up from their listlessness and, with great boldness, they rushed out to tell everyone that Jesus had conquered death and was alive and active again (Acts 4:20).

"Take your New Testament home and read about Jesus' life, death and resurrection in the first four books: Matthew, Mark, Luke, and John. You can read that much in one morning, afternoon, or evening.

"Now, what books do I want you to read?" Peter asked as Gunther and Trevor stood up to leave.

"Matthew, Mark, Luke, and John. Hold my horse while I get on," replied Gunther with a grin.

CHAPTER THREE

At their next meeting with Peter, both Gunther and Trevor laid their New Testaments on the table in front of them and were remarkably quiet.

"Well?" asked Peter, looking them in the eyes.

"I need to read those chapters again," Trevor said.

"Gunther?"

"I have a question, sir. At the start of the Gospel of John it says, 'In the beginning was the one who is called the Word.' It seems to me that John was writing about Jesus. But if he was, why did he call Jesus 'The Word?'"

"Gunther, the Bible is the *Written* Word of God, whereas Jesus is the *Living* Word of God. Now, as I have already told you, the only permanent change for good I've seen in the lives of addicts and folk crippled by bad habits, came about because these folk invited the Spirit of Jesus to come and live in their hearts. His presence there evicted their bad habits."

"So?"

"So, make it a daily habit to prayerfully read the four Gospels—Matthew, Mark, Luke, and John—in the Written Word of God, and Jesus, the Living Word of God, will come into your hearts and bring about the change you are seeking. Will you do that?"

"Well, that's completely new territory for me, but, if Jesus' presence in other people's lives helped them solve their problems, then I am willing to give him a go," offered Gunther.

"What about you, Trevor?"

"Yeah. Me too," Trevor responded.

"That's more like it," affirmed the chaplain. Keep reading and re-reading the four Gospels. That's your primary task. See you both next session."

***

Both Gunther and Trevor arrived for their next session with their New Testaments in hand.

"Good evening, gentlemen. Welcome to our third meeting. Do you have any comments on, or questions about, what you have been reading in the Gospels?"

"I do," replied Gunther with a raised hand.

"Yes?"

"In John 3:17 it says, 'God did not send his Son into the world to condemn its people. He sent him to save them.' Does this mean that the Lord does not condemn me for my faults?"

"It does indeed. That passage insists that Jesus didn't come to condemn you, Gunther; he came to save you. Sin results in eternal death but salvation results in eternal life. Furthermore, God offers you eternal life as a gift, at no cost at all to you."

"A gift? Where does the Bible teach that?"

"Turn to page 246 and find Romans 6:23. Trevor, please."

"Sin pays off with death," Trevor read, "but God's gift is eternal life given by Jesus."

"Jesus died that death in your place, on the cross."

After a few moments thinking about that, Trevor asked, "But if Jesus died for us, why do we still die? Everyone dies, sir. Even Christians die."

"True, Trev. Death is universal. But not everyone lives. Christians, have a mantra that goes like this: *Live once, die twice. Live twice, die once.* Write those eight words in your notebooks."

When they had done that, Peter asked, "Would either of you like to give me your understanding of 'Live once, die twice'?"

"We all live once," said Trevor.

"Who, then, do you think would live twice?"

"To live twice you would have to be born twice," sniggered Gunther.

"Correct. What's another way of saying, born a second time?"

"Being born again?" asked Gunther.

"Yes. Have you ever heard the phrase, 'born-again Christians'?"

"Yeah."

"Now, if you were born the first time into this world, where would you be born the second time?" the chaplain asked.

"Into God's world?" asked Gunther.

"Yes. But what is God's world?"

"It must be a spiritual realm, sir."

"You're getting warmer. God's world is a realm in which there is no death. In other words, it is the realm of eternal life, for all who are born again have eternal life and will never die the second death, because Jesus saved us from the second death. Are you young men saved?"

"According to the Gospels, we are saved if we trust in Jesus," replied Trevor.

"Saved from what?"

"From eternal death, sir."

"That is why a born-again person will only die once. All who have been born again will live forever, for when Jesus returns he will liberate them from death and dying to live eternally with him in Paradise (1 Corinthians 15:51-53).

"I'm now waiting for your explanation of 'die twice,' for those who are born just once will die twice."

"Ahh," said Trevor thoughtfully, clasping his chin, "the only people who will die twice will be those who will die both in this world, and again, when Jesus returns."

"The second death, therefore, will be what kind of death, Trev?"

"Eternal death, sir."

"Precisely. All who reject Jesus' sacrifice for their sins, will die the second death at his coming, which will be an eternal death with no resurrection. We may conclude, therefore, that both the *second* life and *second* death are eternal. If you are raised from your graves to live a second time in your resurrected bodies, from that point forward you will never get sick, old, or die (1 Corinthians 15). On the other hand, those who die the second death will remain dead forever.

"Now, do you know why you won't die a second time?" Peter asked.

"It can't be because Jesus died for us, because the second death is an eternal death with no resurrection. Jesus, however, did not die eternally," asserted Trevor, "because he rose from the dead."

"Oh yes, Jesus did die eternally, son!"

"But he rose from the dead, sir. So, how can his death on the cross be an eternal death?"

"Let's go back to Jesus' last visit to the Garden of Gethsemane," the chaplain said. "In that garden, God gave his Son, Jesus, two choices: If he died the second death in the place of all repentant sinners who had faith in him, then he, himself, would remain dead forever, and they would take his place in Paradise forever. Are you following me?"

"In other words," reflected Gunther, "Jesus would swap places with those of us who believe in him. He—God's Son— would die forever so that we—repentant sinners who put our faith in him— would live forever."

Peter made a circle with his right thumb and forefinger and said, with a slight thrust of his hand, "Spot on. Like the good carpenter you are, you hit that nail squarely on the head. Three times in Gethsemane, Jesus begged the Father to release him from his commission to exchange—with repentant sinners—his own eternal life for the eternal death that they should die (Matthew 26:36-46). Three times the Father declined. So, Jesus, submitting to his Father's will, then chose to die the second death in your place and mine."

"I can't accept that," insisted Trevor, "because Jesus did not die eternally!"

"He did, Trevor. He did!

"On the cross Jesus died the hopeless, despairing death that all sinners will die when they're cut off from God. The darkness that surrounded him on the cross (Luke 23:44) reflected the deep, deep darkness in his soul at that time. This darkness was so intense it totally blotted out the assurance he had earlier: that his Father would restore him to life on the third day. Crushed by the weight of our sins, Jesus was slowly and overwhelmingly sucked into a black hole of extinction from which he could not escape. He experienced exactly what it is like to die with no hope of ever returning to life again.

"No unrepentant sinner will ever experience the torments of hell to the degree that Jesus did that day on the cross because his burden of sin—the iniquities of the whole world from every era—was far greater than that borne by any sinner. And, as the Son of God, he had infinitely more to lose.

"At any moment during this process of being overwhelmed by eternal death, Jesus could have opted out. But he didn't, for he had agreed to die in your place and mine, so he endured this exchange until his life was completely and ultimately extinguished. Jesus, who had come from the highest place in the universe—seated at the right hand of the Father—now, at Calvary, descended to the very lowest place—being totally abandoned by the Father (Matthew 27:46)—which was hell in the most absolute sense.

"On the cross Jesus endured God's wrath against our sin (Romans 5:9). The good news about hell is that Jesus has already experienced the full measure of its torments in your place and mine, thus freeing those who put their faith in him from the requirement to pay for their own sins.

"Now, what I have just shared with you is condensed superbly by the apostle Paul in 2 Corinthains 5:21. Write 2 Corinthians 5:21 (p. 286) in your notebooks, for this is a key text."

The chaplain read the verse aloud: "'Christ never sinned! But God treated him as a sinner, so that Christ could make us acceptable to God.' That's 2 Corinthains 5:21.

"Either we die eternally for our own sins, or Jesus would die eternally for them in our place. So, on the cross, Jesus exchanged his sinlessness (1 Peter 2:22) for the sins of all who put their faith in him. Now, our sin didn't make Christ a sinner, for our sins weren't imparted to him, they were imputed to him, that is, our sin was put onto Jesus' account to be paid for by him.

"Similarly, Christ's sinlessness doesn't make us righteous, for it wasn't imparted to us, it was imputed to us. That is, his unblemished righteousness was put on our accounts, to identify all who believe in him as bona fide citizens of his eternal kingdom. The father's robe did not make the prodigal son righteous, but it covered all his faults and failings with forgiveness and made him acceptable (Luke 15:11-24).

"There on the cross, Jesus experienced precisely what it is like to die with no hope of ever returning to life again. In utter despair he cried out, 'My God, my God, why have you deserted me?' (Matthew 27:46). When God, the source and sustainer of life, turned his back on his Son and walked away from him, life departed with him. At that moment, Jesus experienced the nadir of the second death. With his last breath he cried, *'Tetelestai!'* which is New Testament Greek for 'It is finished!' Then his chin dropped to his chest, and he died (John 19:30)."

"So, what was finished?" asked Gunther.

"In Jesus' day when a debt was paid in full the lawyer would write across it 'Tetelestai' i.e. 'Paid in full'. And when a prisoner had completed his sentence in jail, the Secretary General of Prisons would write across his sentence 'Tetelestai.' i.e. 'Paid in full.'

"So, when Jesus died for our sins, with his last breath, he shouted 'Tetelestai,' (John 19:30): 'Paid in full!'

"All the sins and trespasses that separated us from God were absolved, pardoned and forgiven at the very moment Jesus, with his last breath, concluded his sacrifice. However, because God will not force a single soul to accept his complete forgiveness, he leaves it up to us to either accept or reject his free gift of salvation. To reject his gift of salvation we needn't do anything. However, if we wish to accept Christ's total forgiveness for our sins, all we need to do is accept Jesus as our Saviour from the second death.

"Now, at the very moment Jesus died, the heavy curtain in the temple—the curtain that had separated worshippers from God—tore in two from top to bottom (Luke 23:45), signifying that Jesus, by his death, had re-opened the way for us to enter God's presence and talk with him face to face (Hebrews 4:16), as Adam and Eve did before their fall from grace."

"Whew!" said Trevor when Peter had finished. "I'm going to need a few more runs through that to digest it more fully."

"We'll finish there for today. I'll see you both again tomorrow evening."

***

Before Peter could say anything at their next get-together, Trevor raised his hand.

"Yes, Trev."

"Sir, I'd like some clarification on something."

"Yes?"

"Do the good works that Christians do, such as providing meals for a destitute family, or accommodation for an out-of-luck stranger, have any merit?

"Definitely not, Trevor. The Bible says, 'salvation is God's gift to you. It is not something you can earn, so there is nothing you can brag about' (Ephesians 2:8-9).

"The root of your salvation, Trevor, is Jesus' death for you on the cross. We are not saved because we devote our lives to good works, as Mother Teresa did. We are saved solely by Jesus when we put our faith in him. Mother Teresa will be rewarded for her works (Matthew 16:27), but salvation is not a reward; it is God's gift.

"Furthermore, we are not saved by Jesus and his mother Mary. Nor are we saved by Jesus and his brothers James or Jude. We are saved by Jesus, and Jesus alone.

"Understand, however, that when the Spirit of Jesus—the root of your salvation—comes into your heart, he will produce the fruit of righteousness in your life, which is good works. So, although you are not saved by your good works, you are saved to do good works."

"Thank you, sir."

"Finally, please open your New Testament to page 381 and find 1 John 5:11-12. Have you got it, Trev?"

"You want me to read it?"

"Please."

"God has also said that he gave us eternal life and that this life comes to us from his Son. And so, if we have God's Son, we have this life. But if we don't have the Son, we don't have this life."

"Thank you. Let's explore this verse. Anyone?"

"If we have Jesus, God's Son, we have life," offered Gunther.

"You are already alive so, what is meant here by life?" asked Peter.

"Ah, according to verse 11 it's *eternal* life, sir."

"Therefore?"

"If we have God's Son, Jesus, we have eternal life."

"Yes. Jesus is the *only* source of eternal life. You can neither earn eternal life, nor can you inherit it from anyone. The only way to get it is to invite the Spirit of Jesus into your heart. Do you young men have Jesus in your hearts?"

Both Trevor and Gunther shrugged their shoulders.

"If you believe what you have been reading in the Gospels of Matthew, Mark, Luke, and John, then you *do* have Jesus' in your hearts, because by accepting what the Written Word tells you about God's gift of eternal life through Jesus—the Living Word—you have eternal life.

"I repeat: If you have read the Gospels with a receptive heart, then Jesus has come into you with his gift of eternal life and his transforming power. And that transforming power is what both of you are seeking. Now, I can't have you here for the next two days as I'll have my daughter's two golden Labradorables, Daisy and Mitch, staying with us while she is at a specialist clinic for a minor operation."

"Are the dogs dangerous?"

"Absolutely. They'd lick you to death. They are, however, so nosy they'd be a continual distraction. That break, however, will give you more time to read and absorb the good news of God's saving grace through Jesus."

"Sir, before we leave would you, please, clarify exactly what grace is?" asked Gunther.

"Yes. Grace is God's free and undeserved offer of eternal life. The apostle Paul said, 'We are saved by God's grace, and not by what we ourselves have done' (Ephesians 2:8-9).

"Someone has said that grace is an acronym for: God's Righteousness At Christ's Expense.'

"Grace is the root of our salvation. What we do is the fruit of our salvation. In other words, if you are saved by grace you will reveal it by the way you live. Now, your homework is to focus your attention on the Gospels, which are the first four books: Matthew, Mark, Luke, and John. Read them thoughtfully and read them more than once. Will you do that?"

They both nodded.

"Good. I'll see you on Monday."

***

"Welcome back," said Peter. "Did you have a good weekend?"

"Yes sir."

"Gunther. Do you have Jesus in your heart? Are you a temple for his Spirit?"

"Yes sir."

"Trevor?"

"Sir, reading the Gospels is like opening the lid of a chest full of treasure the very first time."

"That observation, Trev, is very appropriate. In Matthew 13:44 (p.25), a man who was hired to plough a field, discovered a buried treasure. He quickly covered it up, but he had to sell every last thing he owned to get enough money to buy that field, for only when the field belonged to him would that priceless treasure become his. In the same way, you must be prepared to give up everything in your old life in order to obtain the greatest treasure of all: Jesus himself (2 Corinthians 4:7). You have a choice: your old life with its sins, bad habits and addictions, or Jesus and a totally new washed-clean life. You can't have both at the same time. Are you willing to make that exchange?"

"I'd rather have Jesus and a new life, sir."

"Me too," added Gunther.

"Good men. That's a decision you'll never regret."

"Now, I'd like each of you get a clean sheet of paper and write on it all the faults and sins you wish to be blotted out by the blood Jesus shed for you on the cross. Once you have done that, add the word 'etc.', then lightly crunch up your list of sins, put it into a large saucepan, take it outside, put it down on your driveway and set fire to it, signifying that you now walk as free men, rejoicing in God's forgiveness that has completely consumed all your sins and failings."

CHAPTER FOUR

"**T**revor, please give me your interpretation of 'Live once, die twice. Live twice, die once.'"

"Yes, I can do that. If we live only once, that is, our total life in this world, we will die both in this world, and again eternally when Jesus comes back. However, if we live twice in this world, that is, if, after we are born into this world, we are born again into God's kingdom, we will only die once, for Jesus will raise us up to eternal life in God's realm at his second coming."

"Thank you, young man. Well said. Now, because you have accepted Jesus into your lives, both of you should be baptised to seal your relationship with him. Would you like that?"

"Yes, we would," Gunther and Trevor said, nodding their heads.

"Tell me, what do you guys know about baptism?"

"The word 'baptism' means immersion."

"Correct. The New Testament Greek word *'baptismos'* means exactly that. "Jesus was baptised by John in the Jordan near Aenon (John 3:23), because the river at that place was deep enough for him to immerse people. And Philip also baptised an Ethiopian in a pool that was deep enough for him to be immersed (Acts 8:36-38).

"Baptism into the Father, Son and Holy Spirit is a symbol of the whole spectrum of the Christian faith: It's all about replacement."

"Huh?" uttered Gunther with a puckered nose.

"Yes, son. Firstly, Jesus who died and rose again from death, replaced your destiny to die eternally with a destiny to live eternally. Baptism signifies that. Secondly, the Holy Spirit is replacing your old earthly natures with new spiritual natures. Baptism also signifies that. Finally, when Jesus comes back, the Father will replace your sick and dying bodies with new bodies that will live forever (Romans 6:4-5). Baptism also signifies that."

"Sweet as!" Gunther uttered.

The chaplain looked at him sideways.

"Gunther, please repeat what I have just told you."

"Ah. Baptism signifies three things: In the past, Jesus, who died for us, was buried, but conquered death for us and rose from the dead. In the present, the Holy Spirit is raising us up from spiritual death to spiritual life. And in the future, the Father will raise us up from our graves to live eternally with him."

"Capital! Now, where would you guys like to be baptised?"

"There's a small beach, not too far away, in Pullin Cove," suggested Trevor.

"Would that suit you, Gunther?" asked the chaplain.

"Yes, sir."

"When?"

"On the 14th," said Gunther. "It's Trev's birthday."

"You happy with that, Trev?"

"That would make it a very memorable day for me, sir."

***

The day of the baptism was a mixture of cloud and sunshine, with just a light breeze. Trevor, with his family and two fellow workmates from the paint factory, together with Gunther, his parents and his boss, Jim, gathered on the beach of the cove that was sheltered from the open sea.

Peter, Trevor, and Gunther moved slowly out into the water until it reached the bottom of their ribs. "Remember what I told you," Peter reminded them. "Keep your feet flat on the bottom and just bend your knees forward as I lay you down into the water."

Peter, standing side-on to Gunther, held his left forearm across Gunther's chest, and Gunther grasped it with both hands. Peter then raised his right hand to the Lord and proclaimed, "Gunther Adams, because you have accepted Jesus as your Lord and Saviour, I now baptise you in the name of the Father, the Son, and the Holy Spirit. Amen."

Then, placing a supporting right hand on Gunther's back and his left on Gunther's chest, he gently lowered him beneath the surface and then raised him up again.

Gunther, with a huge smile on his face, and with both hands raised high, bounced up and down on the spot, waving to the cheering onlookers. "Sweet as," he said to Peter.

"Sweet as what?" Peter asked.

"Just, sweet as."

Peter then baptised Trevor Davies.

When Trevor stood back up, Peter said, "Happy new birthday Trev."

Trevor smiled. His family and friends cheered.

As they towelled themselves dry, Peter asked, "What's next for you guys. Back to work?"

"I have no job to go back to," said Trev. "I've been made redundant by the new owners of Westcott's. But I'm not complaining because I was given a very good redundancy payment. However, sir, you have given me a totally new focus for my life, so I'm seriously thinking about what I can do to share the good news of salvation with others."

"Yeah, me too," said Gunther.

"But Gunther, your boss, Jim, who paid me to help you overcome your weakness, will be expecting you back on the job."

"I have an appointment to sit down with Jim on the 21st to sort that out, sir."

"That's just a week away. Let me know how things go."

***

Gunther was all smiles when he and Trevor popped in to see Peter a few days later.

"Okay," said Peter to Gunther, "tell me about it."

"Jim told me he had filled in a form to get me registered as a Master Builder."

"You're joking!"

"Nah. But when I told him about my future plans, he said a little bird had told him about my conversion and he wished me all the very best for the future."

"Whew. That's a relief. Now, if you two believe you have been called to share the good news of salvation with others, you will need to spend some time preparing yourselves for this awesome mission. I would strongly recommend that you go to Emmanuel Missionary College near Esk. Emmanuel had a rave review in the Christian press recently. Their next intake of students will be in two months' time, which will give you an opportunity to have a refreshing break beforehand."

"A missionary college?" asked Gunther. "You think we would make good missionaries to people in foreign countries?"

"Gentlemen, there are greater concentrations of unbelievers in our Australian cities and towns than you will find in countries like Bhutan or Mongolia. So, start evangelising here at home. I wish you God's blessing in your new venture. All I ask is that you ring me at least once a month to let me know how you are doing. Will you do that?"

They promised to call him near the end of each month.

"You will be in my prayers every morning," were Peter's parting words to them.

CHAPTER FIVE

After ten days with their families, Trevor and Gunther put their suitcases into the boot of Gunther's car and, full of excited expectation, they drove down the Pacific Highway and turned inland to Esk.

No one they met on the street knew where the college was. Finally, in a second-hand book shop, an old man, whose shirt buttons were done up incorrectly, making one side of his shirt front lower than the other, gave them directions to the college.

While registering and paying their fees, Trevor and Gunther met Geoffrey Clark and Steve O'Halloran from West Australia. They were 'birds of a feather' so they 'flocked together', becoming firm friends.

From that day forward they ate their lunches together, played tennis together and, when possible, they worked together.

They learned that Emmanuel College had been founded by missionaries from Europe. The college operated on an austerity budget. Its only full-time staff were the principal, John Heseltine, a Doctor of Theology; two retired evangelical clergymen with M.A. degrees in theology; a secretary-treasurer, and a caretaker. Two other evangelical clergymen came to teach block subjects, each lasting two months.

Working bees from Queensland churches came for a few hours, twice a year, on rotation, to do maintenance work on the kangaroo, dingo and wallaby-proof fences, and on the limestone road through the property. They also ploughed two small paddocks, in which they planted a variety of melons and pumpkins.

Students were required to work for two hours every day. Gunther was initially employed in replacing a decayed porch railing and the steps on a staff house, and Trevor was made an assistant to the librarian. Other students milked a flock of goats by machine. Some worked in the cheesery, or in the kitchen with Mrs. Vetter in food preparation and cooking meals for the students. And others worked in the laundry, on the farm, in the vegetable garden, or in the orange orchard or banana groves. Every six months they rotated tasks, giving each student the opportunity to acquire a variety of skills.

Emmanuel's purpose was: To teach its students to 'share the love of Jesus with others so that people will become his fully devoted followers.'

The tutorials had just three focal points:

1. The Living Word: Jesus
2. The Written Word: The gospel of his saving grace (in both English and New Testament Greek).
3. The Spoken Word: The sharing of this good news with others in both personal and public evangelism.

In short, their mission was:

a) to **convict** people of their sinfulness
b) to **convert** them to Jesus, and
c) to **commit** them to sharing their faith with others.

At the college they learned how to identify people who were open to the gospel. For example, in a shopping mall one of them would sit down beside a lone person and comment on the nature of the crowd, or the weather. If that person was friendly and willing to talk, he or she would eventually ask the stranger, "Do you go to church?" If the response revealed that they didn't, but were willing to talk further, they'd lead them gently to faith in Jesus.

***

At the end of each month Trevor and Gunther rang Peter to give him an update on their progress. The second time Trevor rang he said, "Hello Peter, Trevor and Gunny here."

"Gunny! Who's Gunny?"

"The students here call Gunther, 'Gunny,' and the name has stuck."

Before hanging up Peter said, "Don't forget to send me an invitation to your graduation."

***

Prior their graduation from Emmanuel, Gunny, Geoff and Steve accepted Trevor's offer to join him in Brisbane. Trevor's maternal uncle Tim, and aunt Nicky McKern had offered him the use of their granny flat for a month, free of rent.

This minor dwelling in the top corner of their section, with its own entrance from a side street, had all the facilities they required: two beds, a double bunk, a kitchen, and a bathroom. It was, however, rather cramped. They would, nevertheless, use and appreciate it until they were able to afford a larger dwelling.

Gunther got a job on a building site with J. K. Hawkins Construction. The job would last only until the flats were completed, but the income would help restore his depleted bank balance. Steve was hired by Chris Wilson as a salesman for paint and painting accessories in his hardware store. Trevor and Geoffrey were, therefore, the only two free to evangelise the community.

On their second day out, they went to a shopping centre. The people there were too intently focused on shopping to have any time to stop and talk to strangers, so they decided to look elsewhere. About midday, Trevor noticed a smaller group of specialty shops on the other side of the road, so they crossed over to check out opportunities there.

Outside 'The Poster Shop', a tall, well-built man in his mid-30s, whose arms and legs were covered with amateurish red and blue prison tattoos, was adjusting the tension of the chain on one of six Harley Davidson motorbikes.

They stopped. "Nice bikes," commented Geoff.

"Nothin' but the best, dude," he replied with both thumbs up.

Geoff put out his right hand and said, "Geoff."

The man with the tats responded, "Carlos," and they shook hands.

"What you guys here for?" asked Carlos. "Maybe I could get it for you at a good price."

"We didn't come here to buy anything," replied Geoff. "We're looking for someone."

"Who?"

"Anyone who feels empty inside and who would like to have a worthy purpose for his life to fill that aching void. Do you know anyone like that?"

Carlos turned his head to look beyond them. "I might," he said whimsically to no one in particular.

"You?"

"Maybe."

"Why?"

"None of ya damned business!" he retorted.

"Sorry," apologised Geoff, who had been eating his lunch on the run. "I didn't mean to offend you. Would you like a sandwich?" he asked, holding out an open paper bag of sandwiches for Carlos.

"They look scrumptious," said Carlos reaching for one. "Yum! That's really nice. What's in it?"

"Our mate Steve makes great sandwiches. "These are salad and egg with a little mayonnaise. Here, have another."

"I don't mind if I do," said Carlos, taking another. "They're moist and very tasty. Where do you guys live?"

"We live together in a small place just over that hill," pointed Geoff.

"You get on well? Living together?" he asked with his mouth half full.

"We don't have any fights, if that's what you mean."

"No disagreements at all?"

"We don't agree on everything, but when there is a difference of opinion over something that concerns all of us, we talk to the Boss about it and eventually we find a solution."

"Who's your boss?"

"Jesus."

"Jesus who?"

"God's Son, Jesus Christ."

Carlos stared at them with a blank look on his face.

"Carlos. We have to go now, as some of us have jobs to get back to. Please excuse us. We'll stop by to say 'hello' again. So, see you later, alligator."

"In a while, crocodile," he grinned.

***

Two days later, Geoff and Trevor stooped at 'The Poster Shop' to say hello to Carlos who was busy polishing his Harley's mudguards and frame with turtle wax.

"Hi guys. Any chance you remembered to bring me some more of your nice sandwiches?" he asked hopefully.

"Yes, we have," Trevor said, passing Carlos a paper bag holding four triangular sandwiches.

"We've also got something even better for you," said Geoff.

"What?"

"An invitation to a men's meeting."

"About what?" he asked cautiously.

"About how to become truly free."

"Interesting. When?"

"Tomorrow, at our place at 7pm. Here's the address," said Trevor, passing Carlos a card with their address written on it.

"I don't know if I'll be able to make it."

"Do your best, mate. I'll be leading the discussion. And everyone's free to ask questions."

The First Meeting

Carlos came and parked his bike inside the gate. Geoff went out to meet him. He gave Carlos a hug, but his response revealed that he wasn't used to another man hugging him. Carlos, however, didn't protest, so that was something.

"We're a bit crowded in here," Geoff said as he ushered Carlos through the door, "so we put our table out back to give us more room."

The others stood and warmly greeted Carlos.

"Okay," said Trevor. "Our time is limited, so let's start. Gunny will begin with prayer."

"Lord," said Gunther, "Please bless us as we open your Word this evening to discover what it means to be truly free. Amen."

"Okay," said Trevor, "our Bible text for tonight is found in John chapter 8, verse 36: 'If the Son makes you free you shall be free indeed.'"

"Excuse me!" interrupted Carlos, "Whose son are you talking about?"

Oh, oh, thought Trevor. *This man is a spiritual infant. We need to backtrack a bit.*

"Carlos," said Trevor, "Jesus is God's Son. He is God in a human body."

"Why did he have a human body?"

"One reason was so he could talk with us, face to face."

"Makes sense."

"And because Jesus is God, Carlos, he has the power to set us free from whatever enslaves us."

"Okay, I can accept that."

"Now, is that promise to set us free universally true?" asked Steve. "I mean, could it be true for a person in prison for murder?"

"Most definitely. He won't be free of steel bars and locked doors. But he will be free of guilt in here," Gunny said, patting the left side his chest. "We are all guilty of something big or small. So, John 8:36 offers all who put our faith in Jesus, freedom from guilt.

"Guilt is a silent killer. It was killing me," said Gunny, "until I learned that Jesus had forgiven me and blotted out my record of sins."

"Excuse me for interrupting again," said Carlos, "but that's too simple. Justice says you should pay for your own sins. Everyone in the clink is there because they are paying for their sins."

"True, Carlos. Jesus, however, offers everyone a choice."

"Yeah! What choice?"

"Either you pay for your sins, or you transfer them to Jesus who paid for them on your behalf."

"So, if I do that, I'll be free of paying the penalty for my own sins?"

"You catch on quick."

"That's too simple. Surely I need to do something."

"You do. You need to repent of all the bad things you have done, and then give them up to Jesus. He'll take care of them from that point forward."

"Again, that's too good to be true."

"It *is* true, Carlos. And the reason we are here is to share that good news with you and others."

After thinking about that Carlos asked, "Okay, how do I transfer my sin and guilt to Jesus?"

"Just ask him to take it from you," said Trevor.

"What? In prayer?"

"Yes."

"I've never prayed," admitted Carlos. "Will you pray for me?"

"If you show that you believe in Jesus by asking him yourself," said Trevor, "he'll answer your request and give you what you need."

Carlos thought about that for a few seconds, let out a long breath, then said, "Whew, man."

"You can do it, Carlos."

There was a long silence.

"Lord, I'm in a right royal mess. Please help me. Amen." He then picked up his helmet and stood to leave. "See you later," he said as he stepped out the door.

"Well," concluded Trevor. "That was short, but from the heart."

The Second Meeting

"In our last meeting, Carlos," said Geoff, "you asked Jesus to help you escape from a bad situation in your life. Tonight, I want to share with you how he will do that in a way that will make you a stronger person."

Carlos raised his eyebrows in anticipation.

"Carlos, if you ask him, God will put his Spirit in you. And his Spirit will give you both the desire and the power to get the victory over your problem."

"I've not seen anything strong enough to overcome the power of the addiction to ice," challenged Carlos.

"Ice? What's ice?" asked Steve.

"Methamphetamine."

"What does it do to people who take it?"

"It turns them into total addicts. To get enough money for their next fix, they become prostitutes, burglars, thieves, bank robbers, or even traffickers of ice."

"Oh man, that's not good. You're selling this stuff?" asked Steve.

"Yeah."

"Where do you get it?"

"I make it."

"Where?"

"The poster shop is our front. While we silkscreen posters there for those who want them, behind the scenes we have a lab that makes ice. And I'm the lackey who does most of the work. I'm trapped in a vicious cycle. It's a whirlpool that is sucking me down and down to my doom. It's stronger than I am, and I can't escape it. What can I do to break free?"

"Well, starting today, we'll all pray that God's Spirit will get you out of the pickle that you are in. So, be alert to his leading and take the opportunity he gives you to escape."

As they stood to leave, Trevor said, "Tomorrow evening Steve will be talking about two people who were building their lives: one was wise and the other foolish."

"Sounds helpful," mused Carlos. "I'm not doing a very good job of mine."

"See you next time," he said as he stood to leave.

The Third Meeting

"Welcome, everyone," said Steve, "and a special welcome to God's Spirit. In Matthew 7:24-26, Jesus told a story about two men: one was wise, and the other foolish. The wise man built his house on a rock. And the foolish man built his house on the sand. The rain came down in torrents, and the wind developed into a gale. The house on the rock stood firm, but the house on the sand collapsed.

"Now, the rock in this story represents Jesus, and the house represents your life. If you, therefore, build your life on Jesus you will survive the storms and problems of life that assail you."

"Whew! Right now I'm caught between the Rock and a hard place," Carlos admitted.

"What do you mean?"

"If Jesus is the Rock, then the boss of my gang is the hard place, for I fear him more than I fear Jesus."

"Carlos, if we gave you the opportunity to walk away from all that, including your Harley, to a better, freer life with us, would you take it?"

"My boss has got me over a barrel."

"What do you mean?"

"He told me, more than once, that unless I continue to make deposits into his bank account, I'll have a serious accident."

"Oh, man. I see what you mean."

"Do you have a solution?" asked Carlos.

"I don't. But I'm sure God does. We will ask him to show you what to do."

"Would you guys please pray for me before I leave?"

That's the first time I've ever heard Carlos say 'please,' Trevor thought.

Trevor and the others gathered around Carlos. Gunny put his hand on Carlos's head and prayed that the Lord would keep him safe in his divine bubble of protection and leading.

"Thanks. I feel more relaxed now. But I've got to go," he said as he stood to leave.

"The Lord be with you, Carlos," said Geoff. "I'll bring you some sandwiches tomorrow."

After Carlos had gone, the group got to their knees and implored the Lord to rescue and bring home this very lost sheep.

***

The next day, at The Poster Shop, as Geoff was handing Carlos a paper bag of sandwiches, a door opened and a husky male voice called, "Carlos! One minute please."

"See you later," said Geoff.

Two days later Geoff went back by himself to talk with Carlos.

"It seemed to me, Carlos, that you'd cut yourself free from your gang if there was a clear way out for you."

Carlos checked to see that no one was in hearing range before nodding and saying, "Yep. I've been thinking about it for some time, but I've never been sure how to go about it, or where to go."

"Right, here's the answer to your predicament. Tomorrow afternoon at one forty-five, go across the road and wait in the bus shelter over there," Geoff pointed. "If the coast is clear, Gunny will pick you up with his car. It's a blue Ford sedan. If you can't make it at that time, he'll wait for you just past the bus shelter."

***

The next day, after Carlos had folded himself into Gunny's car, he guided Gunny to the house in which he had been living with the other gang members, to pick up his bag of clothing and toiletries. Gunny then took Carlos to the minor dwelling belonging to Trevor's aunt and uncle.

The following morning, two gang members came down their street on their Harleys, revving their engines outside their dwelling, making their exhaust-pipes crackle loudly.

"They know I'm here," said Carlos, sucking breaths through clenched teeth.

"How did they know you were here?"

"They've put a G.P.S. tracker on me somewhere," he said. "Could be in my backpack."

"What's that stainless steel triangle on the heel of your right boot?" asked Steve.

"It's probably a brand thing."

"Why, then, is it only on your right boot? May I have look at it, please?"

Carlos took his boot off, and Steve examined it closely.

"If there is anything in the heel, whoever put it in there did a very professional job. Where did you get these boots, Carlos?"

"Last Christmas, B. M. gave all of us new black boots."

"B. M.? Who's B. M.?"

"Black Mamba, the gang boss."

"I have an idea," said Trevor. "Carlos, give me both your boots, please."

With both boots in hand, Trevor went up to his uncle's house. A few minutes later he was back with a broad smile lighting up his face. "I asked Aunt Nicky to weigh both boots separately on her digital kitchen scales. Guess what? This right boot is twenty-four grams heavier than the left one. It's my guess there's a satellite tracker in the heel," said Trevor. "I recommend we should get rid of these boots a.s.a.p."

"We could take them to the truck station just off the highway in the next suburb," Carlos suggested. "Trucks pull in there to refuel. There's a restaurant there where the drivers can get a meal. If we put the boots on one of those trucks, they would be taken on a journey to who knows where. That would give B. M. something to do other than bothering us."

"Tie the boots together with their laces and let's go," urged Trevor. "Gunny, will you take us, please?"

***

Gunny drove out onto the street, unaware that a B. M. gang member was sitting on his Harley in the shade of a tree, up a driveway several houses opposite.

After they had passed, the biker freewheeled down the slope and onto the road, turning to follow them. At the first red light, he pulled up beside them and gave them the finger.

Carlos broke into a sweat. "Gunny!"

"What?"

"What can you do to lose our tail?"

"Not much. A motorbike can go places a car can't."

"Do what you can, Gunny," Carlos pleaded with mounting desperation in his voice.

An idea came to Gunther, but he shook it off because it was too dangerous. *On the other hand, it might just work*, he decided.

When they got a green light at the next intersection, he drove his front wheels to the stop line at the lights and deliberately stalled his car there, even though the traffic light was still green.

Drivers behind him blasted their horns in frustration.

Gunny waited, anxiously drumming his fingertips on the steering wheel. The bikie there beside them with his left foot on the tarseal was glancing uneasily into their vehicle. "I hope that gangster knows that while motorbikes constitute only two percent of the traffic on the road, they have twenty percent of the accidents," Gunny said to the others.

When the two lanes of traffic on their right got a green light and began entering the intersection across his front, Gunny waited until the last second, and then, with his pedal to the floor, he shot across the fronts of the oncoming vehicles whose drivers were now standing on their brakes and leaning on their horns.

When Carlos checked, the gang-member on his Harley was nowhere in sight.

Gunny turned into the second street on his left and then drove down it and turned right into a cul-de-sac where he parked out of sight on the far side of a Morely's Furniture Movers truck that had an aluminium canopy over its deck. It was being unloaded by two men in blue overalls. He waited there while Carlos got out to pee in the gutter, his eyes fixed on the backs of the movers on their way to the house with another load on their trolley.

"Thanks for that," said Carlos as he got back into the car. "I nearly wet my pants back there."

***

At the truck station they found a truck with two large dark green and bright yellow containers, one on its deck and the other on its trailer. After checking to ensure that the driver wasn't in the cab, Geoff tossed the laced-together boots under the container on the trailer. "Let's hope they're off to a distant place like Alice Springs or Darwin," he said, rubbing his hands together. "Tracking them should keep B. M. out of our hair for a while. Now, Carlos, our next stop should be to get you some new footwear. What colour boots would you like?"

"Anything but black. Brown would be nice."

***

At an emporium, Geoff purchased two pairs of large brown elasticised socks and took them to Carlos at the shoe shop where he was examining a selection of brown leather boots with Velcro straps.

Carlos put the socks on, and the boots he had chosen, and walked back and forth with a smile on his face. He then gave Geoff the thumbs-up, so Geoff took the boot-box to the counter and paid for them.

"You are very generous," Carlos said on their way home. "But I'm well able to pay my own way. If you would drive me to my half-brother's place, Gunny, I will pick up some cash I left in his safe for a rainy day."

"What's your half-brother's name?"

"Max Elliot."

"So, you are Carlos Elliot?"

"Yes. Same father but different mothers."

***

Later, Trevor said ominously, "We got rid of that GPS tracker, but the B. M. gang has now discovered where Carlos lives. So, what should we do about that?"

"I have an idea," offered Carlos. "I've always wanted to go surfing on the Gold Coast. I could spend a couple of weeks up there, which may allow things here to cool down a bit."

"Do you have a surfboard?" asked Geoff.

"Yeah. It's under Max's house."

"Problem solved," said Gunny. "I'll take Carlos and his board to the Top Ten Campground at Surfers Paradise. We'll keep in touch by phone, and when we've got ourselves sorted out here, Carlos can catch a bus back. What do you think of that, Carlos?"

"Bonzer, mate. Bonzer."

***

Ninety minutes after Gunny had driven off with Carlos and his gear, two men came to the door and asked to see Carlos.

Geoff asked, "Carlos who? There's no Carlos here."

"We know he's here, mate. So don't try to pull the wool over our eyes. We didn't come down in the last shower."

"Look, come in and have a gander for yourselves. Our place is very small, so it won't take you long to check it out it."

They pushed past Geoff and moved quickly through the flat, opening and checking the bedroom wardrobe and drawers. Having done that, they turned and sullenly stomped off without a word.

CHAPTER SIX

"Chaps, we need to get together for a meeting," called Trevor.

They went outdoors and sat on the low brick wall around a flower garden at the front of the Granny Flat.

"As you know, our allotted time here is almost up. Also, in such crowded conditions, with only one loo and shower, we're getting a bit testy with each other. Furthermore, when Carlos returns, the overcrowding will only get worse, so it's time to move on. But where to?"

Geoff said, "Give me a few minutes to check my laptop to see what's available."

Geoff and Trevor picked three of the best options and Gunny took them to find the most suitable residence.

They finally settled on a third floor, three-bedroom flat with two bathrooms. The only hitch was, the landlord wanted a $2,400.00 bond, which had to be paid into his bank account within 48 hours. Trevor agreed to the terms and signed the rental agreement.

"Where are we going to get that kind of money in a hurry, Trev?" asked Geoff.

"I expect Carlos will come to the party," Trevor replied. "He told me he'd be willing to help us if we moved to a larger place. Anyway, I'll talk to him on the phone this evening to see what can be done."

When Trevor rang him, Carlos offered to pay both the bond and the first three month's rent. "For the first time in my life," he told Trev, "I'll be getting some satisfaction from my stash. It's a strange feeling for me, but I actually feel good about this new adventure. Give me your bank account number, Trev, and I'll arrange for the money to be transferred to you."

"Thank you, Carlos," said Trevor. "You are a Godsend, mate."

***

The real estate agent took them to their new home and said, "Here are three keys to get into the building, and these green keys will unlock the door to your flat. By the way, the keys to the apartment block cannot be duplicated, so treat them like gold."

After Carlos returned home, Trevor said to him, "Mate, you need a new foundation for your life, now that you have chosen to cast your lot with us. You and I should set aside a portion of every morning to study the Bible and to pray together."

So, each morning, before breakfast, Trevor led Calos in several Bible studies about Jesus. He taught him about Jesus' saving grace through his death on the cross. He then taught him about the death and resurrection of those who believed in Jesus. And, after that he taught Carlos about Jesus' second coming and the eternal home of the Redeemed. And so on. Each morning they'd review the previous study before moving on to a new subject.

Three months later, Carlos said to Trevor, "I'm completely blown away by what you've been teaching me from the New Testament. I had no idea that God had such a great purpose for my life, and such a grand future for everyone who puts their faith in Jesus."

At breakfast ten days later, Trevor said, "Most specialist groups have names like *Fire and Emergency*, or *St. John's Ambulance*. We, too, need a name. I suggest that we call ourselves *The Sharers*."

"The Sharers?" the others repeated in surprise.

"Yes, I realise it's not a strong name, but it will evoke a key question like, 'What do you share?'"

"Okay," they said thoughtfully.

So, that's how this team of witnesses got its name.

***

"I don't know about you guys," said Geoff, but I need to exercise every day. "My father once said, 'Geoff, if you don't exercise your muscles on a regular basis, one day they will let you down when you most need them.' So, I'm going for a run every morning before breakfast. And I'd enjoy some company."

Carlos and Steve decided to join a local gym instead. Their personal trainer, Alex, showed them how to use the equipment to stretch their tendons and build their muscles. After each session, they went into the gym's sauna where they steam-cleaned the pores in their skin. They then finished with a barely tolerable cold shower.

A month later, while Carlos was sitting alone in the sauna, he got a nasty shock when the door from the dressing room opened, and he saw B. M. standing there in his birthday suit. Carlos, although mystified, wasn't overly concerned because he was now in peak fitness. Nevertheless, he wondered what B. M's intentions were.

He stood up as B. M. stepped in and turned to face him. Then, as swift as a striking mamba, B. M. grabbed Carlos's testicles, one in each hand.

Whenever Carlos attempted to move, B. M. squeezed so hard Carlos gasped with pain.

"Now, traitor," snarled B. M. "I'm going to ask you a few questions, and if I don't get the right answers, I'll squeeze like this."

"Ah! Ahh! Ahhh!" was all Carlos could utter.

Surreptitiously putting his right hand behind his back, Carlos used his thumb to press his third finger into his palm. Opening his first two fingers like a pair of scissors, and arching backwards, he swung his right hand up and jabbed both fingertips into B. M's eyes.

B. M. shrieked with pain and clawed at Carlos's hand. But Carlos, in one synchronised movement, grabbed B. M's head with both hands and yanked it down into his rising right knee. There was a crunch of rupturing cartilage, and B. M., dazed, collapsed to the floor. Carlos rolled him onto his back, checked his pulse and breathing, then stepped out of the sauna. He was in the process of getting dressed when B. M's sidekick, Jono Basset, who had been exercising nearby, wanting to know why his boss had yelled in pain, came to investigate.

Carlos told him that B. M. had fainted in the heat and almost knocked himself out. "Go in," he insisted. "He may need your help."

Carlos decided, from that time forward, to go running with the others before breakfast.

CHAPTER SEVEN

"**O**ne morning after his Bible study with Trevor, Carlos said, "I wish my half-brother, Max, was here with us."

"What makes you think Max would be interested?"

"We won't know until we ask him, will we?"

"There's no 'we' in this, Carlos. He's your brother, so you ask him."

"But if you come with me, he'll see that you're a normal looking bloke and not a clergyman with a white dog collar. Hopefully, that will make him more open to the good news."

"You think so?"

"Will you come with me?"

"Yeah, I'll come."

"Is Max married?"

"Yes, his wife, Valeria, is from Columbia. They've been married for about four years. But no kids yet."

"How well does she speak English?"

"Very well. No noticeable accent. Val is a secretary for a lawyer who specialises in property sales."

***

Trevor and Carlos rang the doorbell at Max's luxurious home in an upmarket neighbourhood. Max opened the door and stood there a moment looking at Carlos.

"Good to see you again, bro."

"Max, this is Trevor Davies, the man who is helping me turn over a new leaf in my life."

"Very pleased to meet you, Mr. Davies. We are very grateful for all you have done for Carlos."

They shook hands and Max said, with a scoop of his right hand, "Please come in and meet Val."

"Hello, Carlos," she said with a smile. "We've appreciated your phone calls. But they were all too brief, leaving us with lots of unanswered questions. Would it be possible for you and Mr. Davies to come for dinner next Tuesday evening? While eating you can tell us what triggered you to walk away from your gang. Will you come?"

Max, not waiting for confirmation, passed his card to Carlos and said, "If something comes up to prevent you from coming, please give me a ring at this number by Monday evening at the latest."

On their way home, Trevor said to Carlos, "It wasn't what we wanted, so I'll be praying that the Lord will open the door to their hearts at that meal."

***

On the following Tuesday, Max and Val listened attentively to Carlos as he gave an account of his transformation that began near The Poster Shop, and which had been expanding day by day.

"I can't imagine what motivated you to make such an astonishing change in your life," said Max. "I don't believe in this God you talk about. I believe that our universe was created, not by God, but by a Big Bang which started with a singularity smaller than a pin prick, 13.8 billion years ago. Astrophysicists say our universe is *still* expanding."

"That's very insightful, Max," responded Trevor. "However, I firmly believe that the singularity, out of which our physical world came, was created by God who has neither a beginning nor an end. Furthermore, the transformation in Carlos's life, and mine, is a result of the *Spiritual* Big Bang, which began with a singularity containing everything necessary for eternal life to be made available to all who live here on earth. The Holy Spirit placed this singularity into one of the virgin Mary's ova before she and Joseph came together in marriage (Matthew 1:18). The Father of Mary's child, therefore, was God, not Joseph. Her child, Jesus, being the Son of God, spent three years preparing his disciples for when he would no longer be with them.

"On the cross Jesus gave his life as a sacrifice for the sins of the world. He was buried but rose from the dead three days later. Having conquered the grave, he commissioned his disciples to take this good news of God's power over death to the whole world (Matthew 28:19-20) but told them to wait in Jerusalem until they were empowered by the Holy Spirit for this mission (Luke 24:49; Acts 1:4-5).

"Several days later—on the day of Pentecost—they were filled with the Holy Spirit and their mission exploded into the world with apocalyptic power. This spiritual Big Bang produced spiritual life wherever their message of God's grace was received. God himself showed that his message was true by working all kinds of powerful miracles and wonders' (Hebrews 2:4).

"At the Temple the apostles preached to an assembly of visitors from several countries, and each national group heard the gospel in their own language (Acts 2:1-12). Later, the apostle Peter was miraculously freed from a maximum security prison (Acts 12:3-19). The apostles also performed amazing miracles, even restoring the dead to life (Acts 9:36-42). And Agabus, from Syria, exercised the gift of prophecy' (Acts11:27-28).

"Saul of Tarsus, a fanatical persecutor of Jews who became believers in Jesus, had a face-to-face encounter with the Lord Jesus on the road to Damascus: an encounter that turned his world upside down. Blinded by this epiphany (Acts 9:3-9), Saul became figuratively 'dead for three days', during which time he couldn't see, eat, or drink. But, like Jesus, he returned to life on the third day. From that point forward, Saul, who adopted the Roman name, Paul, became the foremost exponent and proclaimer of the Christian faith. Subsequently, Paul founded Christian assemblies in many cities around the Mediterranean. Paul wrote seven letters to these churches, each of which became a book in the New Testament.

"This Spiritual Big Bang is, to this day, still expanding. Though once the gospel was firmly established, the miracles that validated it reduced in number for they had accomplished their task of giving the good news a jump-start."

"That's something I'd like to examine more closely," proposed Max. "You will, however, need evidence more substantial than your 'Spiritual Big Bang' theory to convince me that Jesus is the saviour of mankind."

"I wish to accept your challenge, Max," responded Trevor.

With raised eyebrows Max replied, "I'm willing to give credit where credit is due, so, let's hear it."

"Okay. On the Jewish Day of Atonement, the High Priest took a bowl of the sacrificial animal's blood into the Most Holy

Place of the Temple and sprinkled some of it on the ark of the covenant between the two gilded angels mounted on its left and right sides. This sacred chest, containing the Ten Commandments written on stone, represented God's throne. His Shekinah glory was manifested between these two gilded angels. That atoning blood on the mercy seat thus came between God and these Ten Commandments which condemned all sinners to death.

"Now, after Jesus died on the cross, Joseph of Arimathea and Nicodemus took him down and laid him in a new tomb that belonged to Joseph (John 19:38-41). Three days later, on the day following the Sabbath, Jesus rose from the dead.

"Two female followers of Jesus, not knowing he had risen, went to the tomb to finish embalming his body. At the grave site, Mary Magdalene bent down to look into the tomb. She saw two angels in there. They were dressed in white and sat where Jesus had been laid: one at the head and the other at the foot (John 20:11-12). And between them, the rock platform where Jesus had been laid, was stained with his blood.

"So this is what happened in the temple on the Day of Atonement: The blood between the two angels pointed forward to what would happen in reality after Jesus' body had been laid in Joseph's tomb."

"But why were those angels sitting?" asked Max. "From what I have read, the gilded angels on the ark of the covenant were standing, not sitting."

"Firstly," said Trevor, "They were sitting because the tomb's ceiling wasn't high enough for them to stand up. "Secondly, I understand that it was a common practice for a ruler to sit on his throne to make a judgement (Proverbs 20:8). Moses sat down to judge the people (Exodus 18:13), and Pontius Pilate sat down on the judge's seat to judge Jesus (John 19:13).

"These angel judges, therefore, are sitting in judgment on anyone who despises the sacrifice that Jesus made for them."

There was total silence while Max, Val, and their guests, examined their personal response to Jesus' sacrifice.

"The more I hear about Jesus the more I'm impressed," conceded Val, who was fingering a silver cross hanging on a fine gold chain around her neck. "It seems I still have lot more to learn about him. Anyway, it's time for our desert."

As they finished with a few chocolates, Val said, "Both Max and I are free on Tuesday evenings. Would you be able to come back then?"

Trevor and Carlos looked at each other and nodded their heads.

"Val's more open to the gospel than Max," commented Trevor on their way home.

CHAPTER EIGHT

Two days later, on Thursday, as Gunny was driving Carlos to the supermarket, he kept glancing nervously in his rear vision mirror. "There's a shiny black Beamer following us," he said. "I'll do a 360 around the next roundabout to see if it does the same."

The BMW did.

"That's one of B.M's vehicles," observed Carlos peering out the back window. "It's got his logo on the grill. It's me they're after. I bet he's scared I'll put the cops onto him."

"What'll the gang members do if they catch you?"

"They'll soften me up a little—put me in hospital—as a foretaste of what will happen if I spill the beans on them. Take the next turn left, Gunny, and I'll hop out just around the corner."

As Carlos stepped out, he said, "Keep moving. I'll give you a ring when I'm free."

***

Carlos, feeling vulnerable because of his height, went half-way into a restaurant and sat down at a recently vacated table where he could keep an eye on the front door. He noticed that the only door at the rear—a bifold door with glass viewing panels at eye-level— was on the left. This door gave access to and from the kitchen. If cornered, he might be able to escape that way.

Leaning on the table to make himself as unimposing as possible, he picked up a used cup to give the impression that he had a legitimate reason for being there. His fears were realised when Jono Basset and an unknown accomplice stood in the entrance scanning the customers.

Jono was holding two heavy-duty black cable ties in his left hand. On spying Carlos, they surged toward him, accidentally tipping a circular topped table in their haste. Dishes and cutlery clattered on the floor.

A grey-headed female customer stood up against the wall and began speaking rapidly into her phone. Carlos raced to the kitchen, almost colliding with a waitress carrying out a tray of hot coffees. "You are not allowed in there!" she called over her shoulder.

To the surprise of the chefs, Carlos ran through the kitchen and out a door into a back alley where several yellow rubbish bins stood against the restaurant wall. He tipped them over to create obstacles for his pursuers.

Further on he came to an old woman wearing a dirty, black, floppy hat, sitting on an upturned beer crate. She took a drooping cigarette from her lips and asked, "Who you runnin' from, honey?"

"Some crims," puffed Carlos.

"In there," she said, pointing to a shed full of large blue plastic bins.

Carlos clambered over a bale of laundry, turned a corner, and backed into a space between two stacks of bins. He could hear his pursuers kicking the over-turned rubbish bins out of their way as they got closer.

"Did a big fellow with lots of tattoos come this way?" one of them asked the old woman.

Putting an open hand behind her right ear, the old woman with the dirty, black floppy hat croaked, "Eh?"

"Ugh!" snorted the questioner. And they ran on.

A short while later, the old woman called in a sing-song voice, "You can come out now, honey. They've gone."

Carlos came out, brushing cobwebs off his clothing with both hands. He kissed the palm of his left hand and placed it on the old woman's forehead. Handing her a twenty dollar note he said, "You saved my skin, mum. Big thanks!"

She said nothing but her eyes revealed her pleasure.

Out on the footpath, Carlos joined a crowd that was waiting to cross the road. Outside a shop with a bold street number, he rang Gunny to tell him where he would be waiting. In the distance he could hear the sirens of approaching police cars echoing along the concrete canyon.

When Gunny picked Carlos up, he was eager to hear what happened after he last got out of the car.

"Well," replied Carlos, "I met a beautiful young woman with a pink ribbon in her hair, who found me very attractive. She called me 'Honey.'"

Gunny punched him lightly in the biceps. "Yeah right!" he chuckled.

CHAPTER NINE

The next Tuesday evening, Carlos and Trevor rang the doorbell at the Elliot home.

"Come in. Come in," said Max. "You're on time to the very minute."

Trevor, with Carlos sitting beside him, told his audience the story about Jesus' trial before the supreme Jewish, Council, the Sanhedrin. "The temple guards, led by Judas, and accompanied by a curious mob, arrested Jesus near the Garden of Gethsemane. Peter, feeling very threatened, yanked his sword from its scabbard and slashed at his nearest opponent—the high priest's servant, Malchus—and cut off his right ear (John 18:10). Jesus rebuked Peter, touched Malchus's bleeding head, and restored his ear (Luke 22:50-51).

"The temple guards bound Jesus and took him to the Jewish High Priest, Caiaphas. Caiaphas was still recovering from the shock of hearing Malchus explain why the right shoulder of his robe was drenched with blood. Clenching his fists and jaw, after a long groan, he snapped, 'That man's influence reaches into the very heart of my home! How dare he! I'm the religious authority here! Not him! The sooner we get rid of him the better.'

"The Jews, however, had no authority to execute anyone, so, early next morning, the High Priest and two temple guards took Jesus to Pontius Pilate—the Roman Procurator in Jerusalem. 'What crime has he committed?' asked Pilate? who was feeling miffed at having been called to duty so early in the morning. 'He claims to be a king,' they replied. 'We, however, have only one king, and that's Caesar.'

"'Are you a king?' Pilate asked Jesus. 'If I was a king in this world, my followers would fight to protect me,' Jesus replied. 'But no. My kingdom is not an earthly realm.' Turning to the High Priest, Pilate said, 'I find no fault in him. I will punish him and let him go.' That was a wrong call, for if Jesus was innocent of the charges brought against him, why would Pilate punish him?

"Pilate's unjust decision revealed a chink in his armour that the Jews would exploit to their advantage. A muscular soldier shoved Jesus' face into a canted post, hoisted up the shackles on his wrists and hooked them over a large square-shanked nail protruding from the top, so that Jesus' toes barely touched the ground.

"This soldier, wielding a whip with several thongs, some tipped with small lead weights and others with small bronze hooks, then unmercifully flogged Jesus, bruising and ripping chunks of flesh from his back and sides. He was eventually stopped by his officer who growled, 'You were ordered to punish him, not kill him!'

"Jesus, mutilated, and with a crown a crown of thorns crushed on his head, was then taken up to Pilate who presented him to the murderous Jewish throng in the courtyard below. *Ecce Homo*, ('Behold the man'), he proclaimed in Latin. 'Crucify him. Crucify him,' the hired mob yelled in response. 'Shall I crucify your king?' Pilate asked them. 'Yes!' they yelled in reply. 'Crucify him!'

"Pilate, however, wanting to release Jesus, who was innocent of the charges brought against him, still had one card left to play. He hoped this would be his winning card. It was customary to release a prisoner at the time of the Jewish Passover, so Pilate, wanting the people to free Jesus because he was innocent, addressed the crowd again. 'Who would you rather that I set free: Jesus or Barabbas?'

"Now, Barabbas, a condemned terrorist, was guilty of murder, rape, and robbery. Shortly before his capture, Barabbas and his two cohorts had invaded the mansions of two prominent Jewish merchants and made off with their strong boxes of gold and silver coins. 'Which of these two men do you want me to set free?' asked Pilate again with a smirk, assuming the influential and wealthy Jewish merchants would oppose any attempt to free Barabbas.

"But, urged on by their religious leaders who were so envious of Jesus they were eager to pervert justice, the rabble shouted, 'Barabbas! Free Barabbas!' Pilate then asked them, 'What am I to do with Jesus, who is called the Messiah?' They all yelled, 'Nail him to a cross!' So, Pilate, finally capitulating to the Jews, ordered his soldiers to free Barabbas and then nail Jesus to the cross intended for the chief terrorist.

"Feeling contaminated by his amoral vacillation, Pilate publicly washed his hands in water in a futile attempt to expunge his guilt (Matthew 27:21-26).

"Three crosses had been prepared for Barabbas and his two cohorts. On Pilate's orders the soldiers in the execution squad marched to the city prison. With drawn swords they stomped down the narrow corridor in front of the death-row cells in which the prisoners condemned to be executed were incarcerated. These prisoners yelled abuse at the soldiers and would have grappled with them through the bars but refrained for fear of getting their hands cut off.

"Outside a cell that stank from an over-flowing toilet bucket, the officer in charge of the crucifixion squad called, 'Halt!' He inserted a large bronze key in the cell-door's lock and turned it. The door unlocked with a clunk. The officer then withdrew the bolts and swung the door wide open on its squealing hinges.

"Barabbas, with his arms crossed on his broad, hairy chest, stood in there, defiantly facing the officer across the open space of his cell. Barabbas, a tall, solidly built man, had a thick scar that ran down across his cheek from what remained of his left ear. His nose and ears sprouted tufts of hair, and his lice-infested head was crowned with his hair tied in a knot.

"After staring down this guerrilla leader for a moment, the officer, with a twist of his neck to the left, jerked his head backwards, indicating that Barabbas was to come out. Barabbas sneered but didn't move. 'Out you come!' the officer commanded. 'You're free.'

"'What do you mean, 'Free?'" demanded a disbelieving Barabbas. The officer replied, 'Listen to me you pile of animated dung. Just give me the merest excuse and I'll ram my sword into your guts. You killed two of my mates, and it would give me great pleasure to terminate your life right here and now. So, don't mess with me! You're free to leave because another man is going to die in your place. So, get the hell out of here and have a good wash. You *pong to high heaven*!'

"So, the cross that had been prepared for the guilty man, Barabbas, was laid on the *innocent* man, Jesus, who was taken to Golgotha— the crucifixion site beside a highway where crucified men were displayed to let passers-by observe and ponder the fate of those who defied Rome.

"Now, the prefix 'Bar' means 'son of.' For example, Bartimaeus means 'Son of Timaeus' (Mark 10:46). Likewise, the name Barabbas means 'The son of Abba'. And 'abba' means 'father'. Jesus, the Son of his Father (Mark 14:36), would, therefore, die in the place of Barabbas, the son of his father.

Trevor continued. "You, too, Max, Carlos, and Val—the children of your fathers—have been set free from paying the penalty for your own sins by Jesus, the child of his Father, who died in your place. Will you step forth into the freedom that Christ extends to you? Or will you choose, rather, to remain incarcerated in guilt?"

Deep in thought they stared at the floor.

"At Calvary, Jesus was crucified on Barabbas's cross. And Barabbas's two cohorts were crucified: one on Jesus' left, and the other on his right. The terrorist crucified on Jesus' right was saved from eternal death because he confessed his sins and put his faith in Jesus (Luke 23:40-43).

"Those who are saved are those who, like this repentant terrorist, have also confessed their sins and put their faith in Jesus. The Lord will remember them when he returns in power. Those who are lost are those who, like the unrepentant terrorist on Jesus' left, neither repent of their sins nor put their faith in Jesus. They will not become citizens in the Lord's eternal kingdom.

"Consider now, how Jesus' cross divides the whole world into two: We all line up behind either the felon who was forgiven, or the felon who did not seek forgiveness.

"Who will you line up behind, Carlos?"

"Most definitely behind the repentant terrorist."

"Then Jesus will welcome you into his kingdom."

"I will stand there with Carlos," said Val.

The others looked at Max.

Max shook his head.

"Why not, Max?" asked Val.

"I'm not worthy enough, Val."

"The repentant felon wasn't worthy either, Max. Yet he was saved from eternal death because he put his faith in Jesus who was worthy."

Max shook his head again.

An inspired thought came to Trevor.

"Max. Do you know that you are mentioned in the Bible?"

"Yeah, right!" Max retorted.

"It's here in John, chapter 3," Trevor said as he turned to it. "Verses 16 and17 say, 'God loved the people of this world so much …' That includes you, Maxwell Elliot. God loves you so much, Max, 'that he gave his only Son, so that if you,' Max, 'have faith in him you will have eternal life and never die.' The question now is, will you put your faith in Jesus?"

"And will you, Max, accept that you, the son of your father, Richard Elliot, have been set free from your self-righteousness by Jesus, the Son of his Father?" chided Val.

"Touché," uttered Max wiping his eyes with the back of his left hand.

Trevor, Carlos, and Val stood and gathered around Max. They placed their hands on his head and shoulders, and each prayed in turn that God would flood Max's heart with his forgiveness.

Trevor then sang quietly,

> *Jesus loves you, this we know,*
> *For the Bible tells us so.*
> *No matter what your past has been,*
> *His precious blood has washed you clean.*

Max, with tears running down his cheeks, prayed, "God, please forgive me. I do want to be accepted by you."

"Max, you and Val have made the most important decisions you will ever make," affirmed Trevor. "You should, therefore, ratify your decisions by being baptised into Jesus."

"I don't understand you," questioned Max. "In what way would *baptism* ratify our decisions?"

"Primarily, it will be a public demonstration of your faith in Jesus who died and was buried, but who rose again to life. And through your baptism into Jesus, you, Max and Val will also signify that your old natures have been buried, and the new persons you have become in Jesus, have been raised up to a godly life."

After thinking about that for a while, Val said, "I know a secluded bay down the coast that would be an excellent place for a baptism. The carpark there, however, is very small. But if we all go there early in the morning, in just two cars, we should manage."

"Would you mind if I rang the Rev. Peter Gordon, to ask if he will come and do the baptising?" asked Trevor.

"An excellent suggestion," approved Gunny.

The others nodded their agreement.

On the phone, Peter told Trevor that he and his wife, Sylvia, had been thinking about where to go for a break during the school holidays. He would talk it over with her, after which he would email their answer to Trevor.

Two days later, Trevor received an email from Peter to say that he and Sylvia had booked seven nights in the Palm Court Motel about three kilometres from The Sharers' residence.

***

Down in the secluded bay, Val announced to everyone that she was pregnant with twins.

"Congratulations, Val," they all said as they hugged and kissed her.

Peter put his left hand on Val's shoulder and said, "Jesus, at his baptism, put aside his carpenter's tools and began his ministry to save souls. You, Val, may need to put aside your professional career for a few years to assume the more important role of motherhood."

After Peter had baptised Carlos, Max and Val, they all went to a restaurant, prebooked by Max, to celebrate their baptisms into Jesus with a nice meal together.

CHAPTER TEN

Two days later, Carlos, as usual, went out on his pre-breakfast run. Because the side of the road facing the oncoming traffic that he usually ran on, had long, shallow pools of water on it due to heavy overnight rain, he crossed to the other side, but got a small stone in his right shoe from the loose gravel on the verge.

Someone, hiding behind the mulga bushes growing between two large gum trees on the side he had just left, stood up with a shotgun, aimed it at Carlos, and pulled the trigger as he was bending down to remove the annoying pebble.

The blast struck Carlos in his left shoulder and ribs, pitching him into the roadside weeds.

In the silence that followed, all that could be heard was the distant laughing of a kookaburra and the fading roar of a Harley Davidson's exhaust pipe.

Carlos, thankful for the partial protection of his faux soft leather bomber jacket, crawled back onto the seal and peeled it off to inspect his wounded shoulder. He pulled a clean handkerchief from his pocket with his right hand, spread it over his punctured biceps and held it in place.

His hopes arose when he heard a vehicle coming toward him from the south. As it got closer, it appeared to be a long black station-wagon. Carlos waved his blood-covered handkerchief as vigorously as possible and, as the vehicle pulled to a stop, he saw that it was a hearse with the undertaker's name in gold letters on the side.

The driver, wearing a black suit and bowtie, got out and stood looking down at him.

"What on earth happened to you?" he asked.

"I've been shot."

"Was it an accident?"

"I doubt it."

"Hmm," the undertaker mused, looking around uneasily.

"I've got a body on board that I've just picked up, so you'll have to sit in the front with me."

He opened the door for Carlos.

"Don't worry about getting blood on the upholstery. We have a citrus cleaner that's excellent for dissolving blood that's less than thirty-six hours old. Now, I need to take you to the hospital. Here, let me help you put your seatbelt on."

"Easy, easy, please!" cautioned Carlos with a grimace.

***

At the hospital the undertaker drove into the ambulance bay and signalled urgency with two long blasts of his horn. An orderly came down the steps to talk to the driver. After hearing the undertaker's account of finding Carlos lying wounded on the road, he went around the rear of the hearse to talk to him.

"Excuse me sir," the orderly said to Carlos. "Stay put while I get a nurse to come and decide where you should be taken."

The orderly put Carlos on a bed with wheels and, guided by the male nurse, he took him to the Emergency Department.

CHAPTER ELEVEN

The doctor in the ED gave Carlos a superficial examination and a pain-killing injection in his right buttock. A nurse covered his wound with a temporary dressing, then arranged for Carlos to be taken for an x-ray of his left shoulder and torso.

When Carlos was brought back to the ED, a curtain was pulled around his bed and two men in blue suits came to talk to him. They introduced themselves as Sergeant Mike Colson and senior constable Michael Taylor from the Central Police Station.

They asked the matron if there was an empty room where they could interview Carlos.

A cleaning lady, who overheard them, said room 11a was now ready. They could use that.

So Carlos was wheeled into room 11a where the police questioned him for twenty minutes about his recent past, taking notes everything he said. They asked Carlos for his iPhone, telling him that he could be traced with it.

"I'd like to make a call first," Carlos said.

Taylor looked enquiringly at Colson, and Colson nodded.

"Okay, but make it quick. Do you mind if we wait here while you do that?"

"Not at all," replied Carlos.

***

After bringing Trevor up to date with recent events and assuring him that everything was under control, Carlos thanked the police for their kindness and patience. They then told Carlos they would be giving him the pseudonym of Owen Clifton, which would be used while he was in hospital. He would not be allowed to have any visitors or phone-calls, and was told that the hospital security guard would keep him under continual surveillance. After consulting their superiors at Central, they would return.

***

The next day, the two Michaels came back and told Carlos that the word on the street was that Black Mamba, whose real name was Benjamin Morgan (same initials), had put a price on his head to ensure no other member of his gang would dare follow in his steps.

"You know what that means, don't you?" asked Mike Taylor.

Carlos, who was feeling very sore after having had the shotgun pellets extracted from his body, was, despite the extra oral pain killers, finding it difficult to concentrate.

"No," he replied.

"It means your death must be authenticated. If it isn't, the gang won't rest until the job has been done properly."

"So, how will you prove that I died?"

"Your death certificate will be issued, and tomorrow a notice will appear in the newspaper obituaries column, stating that you, Carlos Elliot, died in the sure and certain hope of the resurrection to eternal life, and that on Wednesday 17th you will be cremated at the Mt. Gravatt crematorium after a private service. Nevertheless, the doctors here assure us that you *will* recover quickly, after which you will be free to leave."

***

The next morning, when Carlos (now known as Owen Clifton), checked the obituaries in the Brisbane Courier Mail newspaper, sure enough, his name, Carlos Elliot ,was listed among the recently deceased.

He relaxed and breathed a little easier.

CHAPTER TWELVE

Six days later, a doctor told Carlos that he was well enough to go home and that he would be discharged the next afternoon.

Carlos was wondering what he should do next when the police visited him again.

Sergeant Mike Colson commented, "You're looking a lot better."

"Yes, I'm now able to have a shower unassisted."

"I've got good news for you," Mike said with a smile.

"I could do with some good news."

"Last evening, in Torres Strait, the Australian navy, in the last phase of Operation Nautilus, arrested several members of the B. M. gang, led by Jono Basset, who were in the process of transferring several plastic containers of cocaine onto their boat from a private Mexican yacht. These men are now on remand awaiting trial. It is expected they will be sentenced to at least six years before parole. You, therefore, have nothing more to fear from them."

"Why was Jono Basset in charge of the group receiving the cocaine?" asked Carlos. "Has Ben Morgan been deposed?"

"Not deposed, Carlos, just indisposed. We understand he's very ill with stage 3 cancer."

***

Carlos was relieved that the B. M. gang would soon be incarcerated. Basset's presence in the Brisbane Correctional Centre would, however, foil a plan he had been hatching in his mind. Carlos, a former crim and jailbird, but now a committed follower of the Lord Jesus, was thinking about offering his services to the prison chaplain to help rehabilitate prisoners. That was something he'd love to do. But the presence of Basset in the prison could make that very difficult. He decided to talk it over with the prison chaplain, Rev. Lloyd Morrison.

Lloyd was very enthusiastic about having Carlos assist him in his work of 'correcting' prisoners. When Carlos revealed his history with Jono Basset, Morgan's 2IC, the chaplain said he would talk to the Warden and get back to him.

A few days later, Carlos received a message telling him that the Warden had transferred Jono Basset to the Sydney Correctional Centre, for he had been in the process of organising his own powerbase among the prisoners in the Brisbane Gaol. It was a case of 'divide and conquer.'

Well, that was a great relief to Carlos, and evidence of God's blessing on his proposed mission.

Lloyd agreed wholeheartedly with Carlos that the only genuine and enduring way to rehabilitate prisoners would be to persuade them to become followers of the Lord Jesus Christ. "However, while you will have some success," Lloyd told him, "the majority will reject your attempts to convert them, for Jesus said the road to eternal life was a narrow road that only a few would choose to travel on."

Carlos was given a form to read and sign:

1. You are allowed only one male assistant, who will need to be approved by the Warden.
2. The only time available for you to spend with a group of four prisoners is Sunday between 10 and 11 a.m.
3. You will be confined to the prison chapel during each session
4. Two guards will be on duty at the door each time
5. Should there be any disturbance, the meeting will be immediately shut down

Carlos signed and dated the document, then handed it in with high hopes.

CHAPTER THIRTEEN

At their first Sunday meeting, four male prisoners: Chris, Tony, Sam and Jake were ushered into the chapel and seated.

Carlos and his assistant, Trevor, sat at a table facing them. Carlos stood up and introduced himself as a former B. M. gang member and prisoner, who had become a born-again Christian.

Trevor introduced himself as a born-again Christian and Carlos's friend.

But before he could utter another word Jake interrupted: "As for me, sweet peas, you can stuff your religion where the sun don't shine and go to hell. I don't believe in this Jesus, so don't waste your breath."

"Jake. You have a heavenly Father who loves you."

"Ha, ha," Jake laughed sarcastically. "A loving father? The only thing my old man loved was alcohol. The welfare grant that he got every week was spent on booze."

"Your mother, Jake?"

"I don't remember much about mum. She packed a suitcase for herself and me, but Dad refused to let me go because if I left home, he would lose the allowance he got for my keep; money he needed for grog.

"When I finished High School, me and my mates realised that if we wanted stuff, we would either have to work for it or steal it. We were too young to get good-paying jobs, so we got into a downward spiral of theft and burglary. After my sixth conviction I ended up here in the clink."

"I sense, Jake," said Carlos, "that you have very little self-worth. If you had God's Spirit in your life, you'd be a totally different person: one you'd be proud of. Have you heard of George Washington Carver, a negro slave in Missouri who grew up at the very bottom of the social ladder?"

"No. And I don't care!"

"Carver's parents gave him the first names of George Washington—the first President of the United States of America—because they had high hopes for their son. They prayed that he'd be filled with God's Spirit, and they weren't disappointed. Because of the Spirit in him, G. W. Carver blessed his country, giving far more than he ever received. If there isn't a biography of George Washington Carver in the prison library, ask your librarian to get one for you. That story reveals what God can do through someone who starts life at the very bottom of the social ladder.

Jake was listening and thinking about what Carlos had said.

Carlos continued. "God wants to make your name—Jacob Harker—also great. But you'll only achieve that greatness if you, like Carver, have God's Spirit in your heart."

"Okay. How do I get that Spirit?" asked Jake humbly.

Carlos went to the whiteboard, picked up a marker, and wrote some capital letters down the left-hand side, one letter beneath the other:

A.
S.
K.

"**A** is for **Ask; S** is for Seek; **K** is for Knock," explained Carlos. "In Luke chapter 11, verses 9-13, Jesus said, 'If you **ask** God for his Spirit, and if you earnestly **seek** God's Spirit, and if you **knock** on God's door to entreat him for his Spirit, he will open the door and give you his Spirit.

"Look at my arms and legs," said Carlos. "I got these tats from a fellow crim, here in this jail. But I am no longer a prisoner to sin. I am a free man in Christ Jesus because I now have God's Spirit in my heart. God's Spirit will come to you also if you earnestly ask for him to come in; if you continually seek for his presence in you; if you open the door of your heart to him and invite him in."

After a long silence Jake said quietly, "I really need God's Spirit, man."

"Are you prepared for the changes he will make in your life?"

"He can only make my life better than it has been," Jake admitted quietly.

Tony raised his hand.

"Yes, Tony?"

"Why would Jesus care about us jailbirds?"

"Tony, when Jesus was asked why he associated with bad people he replied, 'Healthy people don't need a doctor, but sick people do. I didn't come to invite good people to turn to God. I came to invite sinners.' (Luke 5:31-32)."

"That's encouraging, but how do I turn to God?" Tony asked.

"When you are by yourself, Tony, get down on your knees and ask God to accept you as his child. He will accept you as you are, but he won't leave you as he finds you. He'll wash you clean and replace your guilt with forgiveness, and your anger with a peace that will dissolve all your hostility.

"Also, Tony, when the Spirit of Jesus comes into your heart, he will fill that bottomless pit in your life that nothing else can fill. And, bit by bit, he will replace your old sinful nature with the new nature he will give you—a Spirit-born nature that you and he will eventually be proud of. God loves you, Tony, and wants nothing but the very best for you."

"Mr. Davies!" called Sam with his hand up. "There's just one question that I would really like to have an answer for."

"Yes, Sam."

"In this prison we worry about the fact that many of us have nowhere to go when we are released."

"You'd like a halfway house?"

"Yes. That's what we need. A home that will help us in our transition from jail to a better, productive life. So, Mr. Davies", continued Sam, "if, as you say, there is a mighty God who cares about us, I'd really like to see some evidence of this."

"Sam. I'll tell you what I'll do. If you, Tony, Chris and Jake will support Carlos and me by praying every morning for God's help with this project, we will focus all our energies on getting a halfway house for you and other inmates who have finished their time in here but who have no other home to go to. Will you do that?" asked Trevor.

"I've never prayed to God," admitted Jake.

"Praying is just talking to God respectfully as to a good friend. You don't have to get down on your knees to pray. You can pray anywhere. Or get into a huddle and take turns to humbly ask the Lord for new natures. And for a halfway house. Will you four men do that?"

"Mr. Davies and Mr. Elliot!" called Jake Harker. "If you pray that God will fill me with his Spirit, I'll get the lads together every day to pray for a halfway house."

Trevor and Carlos looked at each other and nodded, their hopes rising.

"Come here, Jake" said Carlos, "and get down on your knees and we will ask God to fill you with his Spirit for this ministry."

Carlos and Trevor then prayed that the Spirit of the Lord Jesus would come and fill Jake's heart, thus giving him both eternal life and the commitment needed to lead others in prayer for a halfway house.

"I'll pray for a halfway house too," offered Tony.

"Me too," said Sam and Chris together.

"Fab!" said Trevor, "Your prayers will be more effective if you pray together.

Glancing up at the clock on the wall Carlos said, "Our time here is almost up, so let's close with prayer."

"Thank you, Lord, for blotting out our sins, and for accepting each of us into your family. And please Lord, help us to get a halfway house to help former prisoners re-integrate with society in ways that will be a blessing to all. Now,

> *The LORD bless you and keep you;*
> *The LORD make his face shine on you and be gracious to you;*
> *The LORD turn his face toward you and give you peace.*
> *Amen."*

The prison chaplain, Lloyd Morrison, shook Carlos's and Trevor's hands as they left, and asked them to return to lead other prisoners to a living faith in the Lord Jesus.

As they were leaving, Carlos hesitated and turned back. "Excuse me, Lloyd, have you any idea what's happened to my old boss, Ben Morgan?"

"He was released from prison because he's dying of liver cancer-- probably caused by his addiction to alcohol. I understand he's been given six months."

"Thanks. One more thing, Lloyd. Where do these men go when they are released from prison?"

"If they don't have a supportive family," he answered, "they return to crime. Jail at least gives them shelter and food."

"There is no halfway house here in the city?"

"None that I know of," the chaplain said.

CHAPTER FOURTEEN

On their way home, Carlos said to Trevor, "I believe the Lord is putting the challenge to provide a halfway house for ex-prisoners, on our shoulders."

"That's a great dream, Carlos, but how would we bankroll it?"

"Don't really know. I've almost run out of dosh."

"We haven't yet asked the One who owns the cattle on a thousand hills and the wealth in every mine," admitted Trevor.

"Help us, Lord!" begged Gunther. "Please, Lord, help us get a halfway house to help these men transition into society after they have been released."

***

On their next visit to the prison, Trevor said to Lloyd, "I believe Jake has given his heart to the Lord."

"Prisoners are great actors," he replied, "and they'll assume any guise which they believe may reduce their time in the clink."

"What can be done to test his sincerity?"

"Leave it to me. I'll need two days."

On the first day, Lloyd asked a guard to secretly put two cigarettes in Jake's cell while he was in the shower, and on the second day, two marijuana leaves.

Both the cigarettes and the marijuana had been taken from visitors who were attempting to smuggle them into the prison.

While Jake didn't smoke, cigarettes and marijuana were great currency in any jail.

Both times, Jake handed the illicit drugs in, so the chaplain gave him his tick of approval.

CHAPTER FIFTEEN

With some trepidation, Carlos and Trevor knocked on Ben Morgan's door. His housekeeper opened it and looked at them. When they told her they had come to see Ben, she invited them in.

Around the kitchen table she told them that the District Nurse came at 10.30 a.m. three times a week to sponge Ben on a rubberised sheet, check his blood pressure and oxygen level, and administer his medications.

"Wait here," she said, "while I go and see if he is in a suitable state to have visitors."

A few minutes later the housekeeper returned and said, "He's awake. When I told him you were here to see him, he perked up and said, 'Bring them in.'"

She shrugged her shoulders and said, "Follow me," then, leaving them at Ben's bedside, she returned to the kitchen.

***

Ben was mere shadow his former self. His eyes were bloodshot, his skin was grey, his cheeks were sunken and his nose was bent.

"Hello Carlos," he smiled faintly. "Back from the dead, I see. So, that was a bogus death, eh?"

"Yeah, boss. I grieve to see you like this."

"Why are you here?" Ben asked.

"I heard you had terminal liver cancer, and although I dislike you, Ben, I really feel sorry for you."

"You're the only one who does. But now that you are here, I would like you to do something for me. I believe I can trust you because I've heard that you've become a dinkum Christian. Is that correct?"

"Yes, Ben. Jesus is my new Boss."

"Okay. Carlos, I want my money to be used for the benefit of prisoners who have no home to go to after they are released from jail. If you will promise me—hand on heart—that you will ensure this happens, I'll get my lawyer, Sidney Angelson, to give you what is necessary to provide a Supported Living Home for released prisoners. He'll give you what you need, but don't waste it, for I want Mrs. Ryan, my housekeeper, to have enough to brighten her retirement."

Carlos stood to attention and, after placing his right hand on his heart, said sincerely, "Ben, I promise to follow your instructions to the letter. So, help me, God."

Then, looking directly into Ben's eyes, Carlos asked, "Ben, would you consider accepting Jesus as your Lord and Saviour?"

Ben smiled, snorted faintly, and shook his head weakly but determinably.

***

Sidney Angelson told Carlos and Trevor they wouldn't get a single cent until they had found a suitable home for released prisoners and the City Council had rubber-stamped its proposed use.

On their way home from the lawyer, Trevor asked Carlos, "When we get a house, who will we choose as a live-in supervisor?"

"I know only one person who qualifies for that job," said Carlos, "and that's Jake Harker. He not only understands how prisoners think, he has also been born again by God's Spirit."

"But Jake hasn't been born by water, Trev. Jesus said in John 3:5, we must be born by both the Spirit and by water. And Jake hasn't been baptised!"

"Uh, oh. I slipped up."

"I'll give Lloyd a ring and ask him if there is any way we could baptise Jake before his release."

***

When Trevor rang the prison chaplain, Lloyd told him that the Assemblies of God Church had a portable long, narrow fibreglass tank that they used for baptising born-again prisoners. It was only big enough to hold the person who was to be baptised, so the one doing the baptising had to lower the convert into the water while standing outside the tank.

Lloyd offered to ask the AOG's for permission to use it.

A fortnight later, Trevor and Carlos found a suitable house, but the neighbours successfully persuaded the City Council to deny ex- prisoners the right to live there.

Over a meal of fish and chips, Trevor mused, "Jake has been baptised, but we have not yet found a home that we could renovate for our purpose. For three weeks we have been searching for a suitable home, but we've made no progress. So, I suggest we go back to the drawing board and look at an alternative to a house."

Eventually, they found a Warehouse on the edge of the city that had a large yellow For Sale sign on its front wall.

This building had two offices, a kitchen and a toilet upstairs. On the ground floor was a parking area for four vehicles, a storage area for merchandise, plus room for rubbish bins and other things.

The Halfway House Board, consisting of Trevor Davies (chair), Gunther Adams, Carlos Elliot, and Lloyd Morrison, after agreeing on the site, went to Sidney Angelson with this proposition.

Angelson approved their choice of building, and engaged architect Vern Lewin, to draw up the plans for the interior renovations. Six single bedrooms would be built upstairs. A tiled bathroom with three showers, two toilets with three individual urinals would be constructed on the ground floor. The tilting door to the ground-floor carpark would be replaced with a wall and a strong, wooden front door, wide enough to get furniture into the house.

***

Builder, Rob Gilet, with his team of carpenters, and sub-contracted electrician (Gilet's son), working together with a plumber, completed the project before winter.

Everyone involved in the renovation was then given a printed invitation to a Thanksgiving Banquet—to be held in the completed structure—financed by the lawyer with funds from Ben Morgan's legacy.

At 2pm. on a drizzly Monday, invitees parked their vehicles on the roadside and assembled outside the building, with their umbrellas up, for the opening ceremony.

Lloyd Morrison and his wife Julia, wearing smart raincoats with hoods that sparkled with rain drops, mingled with the invited guests.

"Looks like the showers are easing," commented Lloyd to Carlos as a ray of sunshine lit up a tree-covered hill in nearby Pankhurst Park.

Mayor Charles Whittaker, after a short speech, reached for a tassel on a dangling white cord and tugged it. The flag fell free to reveal a nameplate with GOBORN HOUSE in polished brass letters set in red enamel.

***

While sipping a glass of sparkling fruit-juice punch and eating an apple slice in the large, indoor area on the ground floor, the mayor turned to Carlos—who was wearing long trousers and a long-sleeved, red-checked shirt—and said to him, "I'm puzzled, Mr. Elliot, by the name you have chosen for your halfway house."

"I can't tell you too much," replied Carlos, "but it's in honour of a major sponsor who wishes to remain anonymous."

"I thought the whole project had been paid for?"

"That is true of the property and the building with its basic equipment, such a table with four chairs, an electric kettle, a small refrigerator, and an electric bar heater. Morgan's legacy also covered the cost of renovations to the building's interior, such as the installation of a kitchen, six bedrooms and ground floor toilets.

"Nevertheless", said Carlos, consulting his list, "the kitchen needed a workbench, a pantry, storage drawers and cabinets, a dishwasher, a microwave, a double-door refrigerator, and an oven. And we purchased baking pans, fry pans and pots for the kitchen, and a longer table with eight chairs for the dining room, plus crockery, cutlery, and tablecloths. We also had an air conditioner installed, and a washing machine. We purchased a light-weight Dyson vacuum cleaner, and we needed beds for six bedrooms, bedside-cabinets, mattresses, pillows, pillowcases, sheets, blankets, and towels for the bathrooms.

"Additionally, there will be Council rates, insurance, depreciation and contingencies, building-maintenance, the superintendent's wages, gas, water and electricity bills, food, laundry, Dentists and doctor's bills, and sundry items."

"Yes, of course," replied the Mayor. "You know, with these parameters that you have defined, this venture could be replicated in other cities, for, with the right in-house supervisors, such halfway houses will considerably reduce recidivism, which will be better for both inmates and the national budget."

***

"Excuse me please, Carlos."

"What is it, Gunny?"

"Notice has just come in that Jake Harker is to be released at 10.30 a.m. next Monday week."

"Thank you, Lord," said Carlos, looking upwards. "Will you pick him up, Gunny?"

"I've already got it in my diary. And I've just asked the chaplain to tell Jake I'll be waiting for him."

"Thanks. That reminds me, I need to get a Supervisor sign for his office door."

***

"I've been thinking," said Trevor, "that I should move in for a week or two with Jake and the first residents, to help get the ball rolling with 'the family.' You know, starting the day with a Bible reading and prayer, checking appointments for the day, and inhouse duties like cooking, vacuum-cleaning, laundry and dishwashing.

"We should also get some HOUSE RULES signs printed. But first we will need to have a meeting of the Board to decide what rules will be essential. Please run your eyes over my proposed list."

Gunny, glanced at the list Carlos had hand-written.

HOUSE RULES

No alcohol or recreational drugs

No smoking or vaping

All visitors must sign in when they arrive and sign out when they leave

No visitors after 9 p.m.

No noise after 9.30 p.m.

Weekly room inspections

"We could also ask for volunteers to come here to teach literacy to help these men become good readers and writers, and others to help them get their driver's licences for various types of vehicles and machinery."

At that moment, a tall and striking young woman with a pink ribbon in her straw-coloured hair caught Carlos's eye. She smiled and stepped towards him in her classy black boots. "Hello Carlos," she said, as she opened her purse and extracted a business card. "I am an evangelical Christian, and I believe I can be of personal help to you with your project," she continued as she handed her card to him.

Carlos noticed that her first name was Brooke.

"How personal, Brooke?" asked Carlos.

"That's up to you, honey," she said with a smile as she turned and departed, leaving Carlos gazing after her.

As Carlos reached for a sausage roll, he saw, out of the corner of his eye, Brooke taking the pink ribbon from her hair and giving it to Gunny, who had a grin from ear to ear.

"Why, you!" shouted Carlos, running at Gunny, winding up to punch him on the shoulder.

But Gunny, chortling at his joke, turned and fled.

"If only," thought Carlos in his disappointment. "If only her offer had been genuine. Ah, well, those sausage-rolls are very tasty. I think I'll have another."

As he reached out for one, he caught a whiff of perfume and turned to see who it was, hoping it would be Brooke. It was.

"You really had me there," Carlos told her.

"Yes, it was supposed to have been a prank, but I'm very grateful to Mr. Adams for introducing me to you, even if it the introduction was a bit unconventional. Would you mind if I got in touch with you again? I'd like to do that."

"Mind?" exclaimed Carlos. "I can't wait!"

***

Carlos, full of hope, and thrilled about the growing success of their God-given mission of helping to convert the worst people into the best people, now, unable to contain his overflowing joy, ran to the rear of GOBORN HOUSE and shouted, "Hallelujah!" so loudly that a flock of Barbary doves that had been feeding on wild bird seed scattered there by an old lady wearing a black, floppy hat, took to the air on whirring wings.

"Praise God!" she echoed. "Praise God!"

"Hallelujah!" Carlos shouted again and again with raised hands. "Thank you, Lord. Thank you. Thank you. Who can put a value on all your blessings? They are priceless. There's no Boss like you! None! Absolutely none! Hallelujah!"

finis